BABY CHOMPER'S
BATH TIME

nuggies™

Story by Jeff Minich
Illustrated by Renan Garcia

Published in the United States by Nuggies.
Park City, Utah

ISBN: 978-0-9992984-0-4

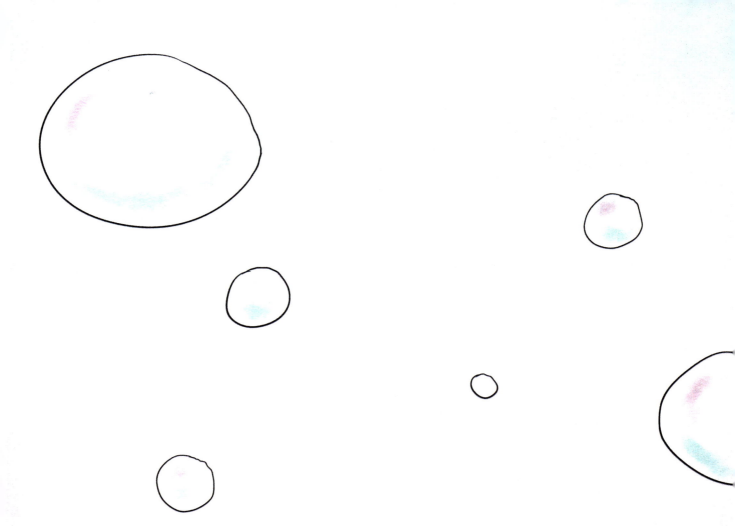

Visit us at:

www.getnuggies.com

When you smell this bad
the only thing to do
is take a nice long bath!

But if there is one thing Chomper really doesn't like, that one thing is...

When it's time to wash up
you have to get in the tub.

But taking a bath
doesn't have to be so bad
if you stop and think about
all the fun you can have.

Or set sail across the sea...

and be the captain of a ship!

Or surf a giant wave...

all the way into shore.

With a little imagination...

you can do all this and more!

After a little rub a dub dub dub...

baby Chomper is all freshened up!

So fresh!

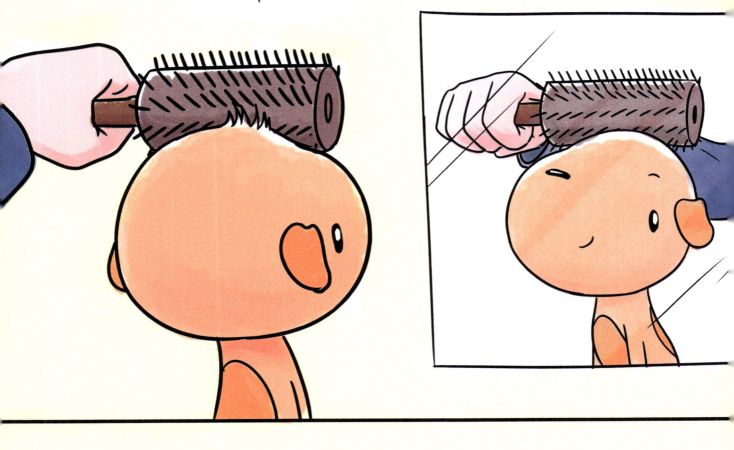

Freshy fresh!

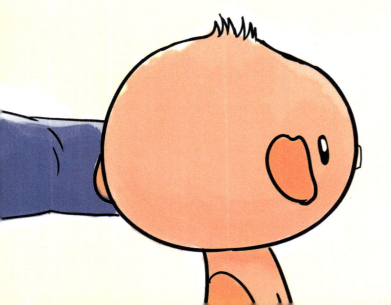

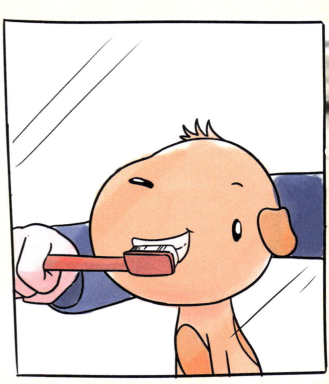

Before Chomper knew it, bath time was done.
And this bath time taught him that
even things you don't like can still be big fun!

CPSIA information can be obtained
at www.ICGtesting.com
Printed in the USA
LVOW05*1914270218
568087LV00006B/8/P